Sister climbed the stairs to the attic. When she reached the door, she got something of a shock. She was used to seeing Gran in her usual plain housedress. But instead, there was Gran dressed in the costume of Wanda the One-Bear Band. She wore a pink-spangled body suit and had all of the one-bear-band rig—harmonica, saxophone, drum with cymbals, and bicycle horn. She was even wearing roller skates!

BIG CHAPTER BOOKS

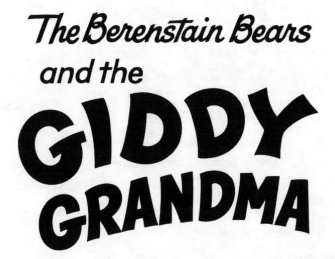

The Berenstain Bears and the GIDDY GRANDMA

by Stan & Jan Berenstain

A BIG CHAPTER BOOK™

Random House New York

Library of Congress Cataloging-in-Publication Data
Berenstain, Stan.
The Berenstain Bears and the Giddy Grandma /
by Stan and Jan Berenstain.
    p. cm. — (a Big chapter book)
SUMMARY: Sister Bear interviews her grandmother for a school assignment, Gran decides to enter her old vaudeville act in the school talent show, and Gramps moves into the gardening shed.
ISBN 0-679-85814-8 (pbk.) — ISBN 0-679-95814-2 (lib. bdg.)
[1. Bears—Fiction. 2. Schools—Fiction. 3. Oral history—Fiction.
4. Grandparents—Fiction. 5. Talent shows—Fiction.]
I. Berenstain, Jan. II. Title. III. Series: Berenstain, Stan.
Big chapter book.
PZ7.B4483Beffe 1994
[Fic]—dc20 94-11469

Manufactured in the United States of America 10 9 8 7 6 5 4 3 2 1

BIG CHAPTER BOOKS is a trademark of Berenstain Enterprises, Inc.

Contents

Chapter 1
The History Project

It sure isn't just the same old stuff, thought Sister Bear as she and Brother turned into the driveway of the Bears' tree house on their way home from school. The new history project that Teacher Jane had assigned for homework was not like any project Sister had ever done. At first she wasn't sure she could handle it. But the more she thought about it, the more interesting it seemed. She wanted to give it her best try.

1

Papa Bear looked up from his afternoon newspaper when the cubs came into the living room. "Well," he said, "what happened in school today?"

"Nothing much," said Brother. He took off his backpack and raced upstairs. Soon he came racing back down with his basketball tucked under his arm. "Gonna go shoot some hoops with Cousin Fred," he said. "See you later." And in a wink he was out the door. Sister just stood there lost in thought.

Mama looked up from the book she was reading. She wondered what was on Sister's mind. Sister usually answered Papa's question as quickly as Brother did. But she hadn't said a word yet.

"Did something unusual happen?" asked Mama.

"Kind of," said Sister. "Teacher Jane gave

us a history project for homework."

"What about?" asked Papa.

"Bears," said Sister.

"Bears?" said Papa. "Oh, you mean famous historical figures. What kind? Presidents? Generals? Pioneers? Inventors?"

"None of those," said Sister.

"What else is there?" said Papa, frowning.

"Ordinary bears," said Sister. "Plain old ordinary bears."

"Plain old ordinary bears," Papa repeated. He pretended to look worried. "Tell me, Sis—has Teacher Jane been feeling all right lately? Been complaining of headaches, dizzy spells...?"

"Oh, stop it, Papa," Mama scolded. Then she turned back to Sister. "What exactly did Teacher Jane say about these plain old ordinary bears?"

"She said that there's more to history

HAS TEACHER JANE BEEN FEELING ALL RIGHT LATELY?

than what's in our history books," said Sister. "More than all the stuff about famous historical figures like Papa mentioned. She said that what happens to ordinary citizens of Bear Country is history too."

"Hmm," said Papa. "I've never looked at it that way. Sounds good. Except for one thing. You might have trouble finding history books about ordinary citizens."

"That's why it's going to be an *oral* history project," said Sister. "I'm supposed to interview an ordinary citizen and record the events of their life on tape. Then I'll give a talk about them to the class. Teacher Jane told us to pick an older bear to interview. That's because older bears have more to tell. Their memories go further back in history."

"That's a great idea," said Papa. "Who are you going to interview?"

"Well," said Sister, "I thought maybe you or Mama."

"Me?" said Papa. "No way. I'm not old! I'm in the prime of life!"

Mama said, "I think Teacher Jane probably meant someone older than Papa and me, dear."

"Oh," said Sister. "That makes it harder. I don't really know any old bears."

"What about Gran?" said Mama.

Sister could hardly believe her ears. "Gran?" she said. "Now, I love Gran, of course. But she's just my grandmother. What could possibly have ever happened to Gran? It's got to be somebody *interesting*. And Gran is just...well, just Gran."

Mama smiled. "I think, dear, you should talk to Gran about this before you decide whether or not she's interesting."

Just then Brother opened the front door

and came into the room. He had a glum look on his face and beads of water all over him. "It's raining," he said.

"So it is," said Papa, suddenly noticing the sound of raindrops on the tree house roof. "Where's your basketball, son?"

"It got wet, so I left it in the yard," said Brother. Then he reached into his back pocket and took out a folded piece of paper. "By the way, here's a notice from school." He handed it to Mama.

"I've got one too," said Sister. She took it out of her backpack. "Here."

After Mama read the notice, she asked the cubs if they had read it yet. Brother and Sister both shook their heads.

"Well," said Mama, "Bear Country School's big fund-raising event this year is going to be a parent-teacher talent show in

PARENT-TEACHER
TALENT SHOW

April 14 - School Auditorium
OPEN TO ANYONE OVER 21

VALUABLE PRIZES!

- Dinner for 2 at the Bear
  Country Inn
- $100 Bear Mart gift certificate
- A case of Farmer Ben's Boysen-
  berry Honey
- A brand-new color TV
- A complete home computer
- A week for two at Grizzlyland

the school auditorium. A number of Bear Country businesses have donated valuable prizes for the winners. What do you think of that?"

Brother shrugged. "What talent could teachers have?" he said.

"Or parents?" added Sister.

"You'd be surprised," said Mama. "I happen to know that Teacher Jane is a great tap dancer. And Queenie McBear's mom plays the flute."

"Hey!" said Papa, looking at the notice. "With great prizes like these, you don't have to look any further than this house for grown-up talent. I might enter and do my amazing card tricks!"

Papa jumped up. He dashed to the bureau and took a deck of cards from one of its drawers. "Now get a load of this," he said proudly. He tried to accordion them

from one hand to the other the way gamblers do. Every last card ended up on the floor.

"Sure," said Mama, bending over to pick up the cards. "And I might enter *my* talent: picking up all the stuff Papa spills!"

The cubs got down on hands and knees to help Mama. But Papa wasn't done showing off. Suddenly he grabbed Mama and started to do a wild tango. "Dancing!" he cried. "That's our *real* talent!"

At first Mama held back. But then she went along with Papa, laughing all the while.

"Or," said Papa, "maybe the twist!"

Both laughing, Mama and Papa began twisting their hips back and forth while pumping their fists like boxers.

"The *what?*" asked Sister.

"The twist!" said Papa. "It's a dance we used to do when we were teenagers."

Now Brother and Sister began to laugh too. Mama and Papa twisted until they fell on the sofa laughing. By that time the cubs were so far gone they were rolling around on the floor, shrieking with laughter. Sister

11

laughed so hard her sides began to ache.

When she had finally calmed down, Sister lay exhausted on the floor. As she looked up at the ceiling, a thought suddenly popped into her head. Maybe old bears did have some kind of life long ago when they were young. Maybe Gran would be a good subject for her oral history project, after all. And after school tomorrow might be a fine time to talk with her about it.

Chapter 2
Some Doubts About Gran

But at school the next day, Sister began to wonder again if Gran would really be a good choice for the history project. The other cubs' choices all seemed much more interesting.

Lizzy Bruin was going to interview an uncle of hers who was a famous brain surgeon in Big Bear City. Queenie McBear chose her Aunt Minnie, who had won the Bear Country Marathon three times. And Tim Honeypot was planning to interview an important politician—his great-uncle, Mayor Horace J. Honeypot.

Gran was no brain surgeon. She had never won a marathon. And she didn't hold an important political office—or even an *unimportant* one. Gran was...well, just Gran.

Sister thought the problem over all day in school. By the end of the day, she wasn't at all eager to interview Gran. But she knew that Mama had already told Gran she would visit after school to get help on a school project. So as soon as school was over, Sister set out for Gramps and Gran's house.

She found Gran on her hands and knees in the garden, hard at work.

"Hi, sweetie!" said Gran. She stood up and took off her gardening gloves, then gave Sister a hug and a kiss. "Your mom said you need a little help with a school project. Whatever it is, I'll be glad to help."

"It's more like a *lot* of help," said Sister.

"So much the better," said Gran. "Is it about gardening? I know a lot about gar-

HI, SWEETIE!

dening. Roses are my specialty. But I'm pretty good on pansies and petunias too."

"It's not about petunias, Gran," said Sister.

"Then it must be about cooking. I'm on firm ground there too. Why, I've got recipes—"

"No, Gran," said Sister. "It's about *you*."

Gran looked very surprised. "Me? Little old *me*?"

"That's right," said Sister. "And 'old' is an important part of it."

While Sister described the oral history project, Gran put her gloves back on and finished putting some small pink-flowered plants in a soft bed of earth. Sister picked up the watering can and sprinkled the plants as Gran planted them.

"Sounds like a fine project," said Gran over her shoulder when Sister was finished talking. "I like the idea of recording the events of the lives of ordinary citizens. Tell me, what's going to happen to all those 'lives' after you and your classmates collect them and give your talks?"

"I'm not sure," said Sister. "Teacher Jane said something about gathering all the tapes together and maybe putting them in the Bear Country Library."

"Great idea," said Gran. "I happen to be

on the library board. Maybe I can help with that." Then she set down her gardening tool and got a far-off look in her eyes. Sister could tell she was going way back in her memory. It was the same look Mama and Papa got whenever they were about to tell something that happened long ago. And some of Mama's and Papa's stories were very interesting.

Hmm, thought Sister. Maybe Gran's oral

history isn't going to be so boring, after all.

Now Gran was putting the last of the plants in the ground. "Do you know what these plants are called?" she asked Sister.

" 'Patience,' I think," said Sister. "We have some at home."

"That's close," said Gran. "The correct name is '*im*patiens,' " She chuckled. "That was me when I was young—*impatient*."

"Should I start my tape recorder?" asked Sister.

"No," said Gran. She stood up. "Let's go inside for some milk and cookies. I've got some fresh-baked ones."

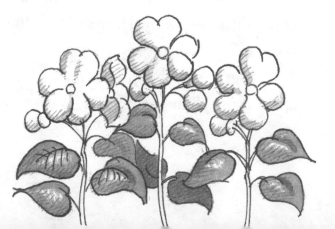

Chapter 3
Grumpy Gramps

Grizzly Gramps was sitting in his rocking chair in the living room, reading the newspaper. At first he didn't see Gran and Sister come into the room. He was frowning as he read.

"Dang school board! Always looking for more money!" he grumbled. But as soon as

he saw Sister, his whole face lit up. "Well, well, what a pleasant surprise," he said. "Come over here and give your old Gramps a hug."

Sister gave him a big squeeze around the neck. "What are you so mad about, Gramps?" she asked.

"Dang school board," said Gramps. "Always needs more money. What are you cubs doing at that school? *Eating* those blackboards and chalk?"

Sister giggled. "Hey, don't worry, Gramps. They're gonna put on a big parent-teacher talent show to raise money. Will you buy some tickets?"

"I'll buy 'em," said Gramps. "But I won't go."

"Why not?" asked Sister.

"Watching folks who should know better make fools of themselves gives me the itch."

Gran said, "Oh, everything gives you the itch. Come on, Sister. We've got work to do."

"What kind of work?" asked Gramps.

"I'm going to tell our granddaughter the story of my life," said Gran proudly.

"Ha!" snorted Gramps. "*That'll* take about two minutes!"

"Humph!" said Gran. "Sometimes *you*

give *me* the itch."

Gramps grinned as Gran and Sister headed for the kitchen. Ha ha, he thought. Tell her whole life story in two minutes. *That* was a good one.

But when the kitchen door had closed and he was alone again, Gramps got that same far-off look in his eyes that Gran had gotten earlier. And his grin gave way to a worried look.

Chapter 4
Gran's Attic

Sister sat right down at the kitchen table for her milk and cookies. But instead Gran put them on a tray and said, "Come on. And bring your tape recorder."

"Where are we going?" asked Sister.

"On a trip into the strange and mysterious past," said Gran. "Up into that time tunnel known as 'Gran's Attic.' "

They climbed to the second floor, then made their way up a rickety stairway to the attic. Sister had never been there before. It *was* a sort of time tunnel, piled high with interesting-looking old things. There were old TV sets, old-fashioned record players,

old furniture and window screens, and ten-nis rackets with holes in them.

Gran put her hands on her hips and looked around the musty room. "Downstairs is where Gramps and I live," she said. "Up here is where our *past* lives."

Sister cleared off a space on a dusty old card table for her tape recorder and switched it on. She took a bite out of one of Gran's home-baked chocolate chip cookies. "Mmm!" she said. "These are great." She took another bite and chewed happily. "Gran, what did you mean earlier when you said you were 'impatient'?"

"Just that," said Gran. "Never liked to wait for things to happen. Wanted to *make* them happen. Wanted to get on with my life. Quit school, for instance."

Sister gasped and opened her eyes wide. "Didn't you graduate from high school? And

DIDN'T EVEN *START* HIGH SCHOOL, DEAR.

what about college?"

Gran gave a wistful smile. "Didn't even *start* high school, dear," she said. "As for college—well, not as many folks went to college in those days. It was different back then. Didn't have television. Radio was the big thing. Some cars still had to be started with a crank—like big windup toys. Didn't have automatic washing machines or anything of the sort."

No TV, thought Sister. It was a hard thing even to *imagine.*

"Yep," said Gran. "I quit school and got a job as a cashier at the local vaudeville theater."

"Vaudeville?" said Sister.

"It was like the movies, only with live entertainment. You know—singers, dancers, comedians, acrobats. Worked my way up, helped out, cleaned up, worked the curtain. Then I became assistant to the headliner, or star of the show. She was what was called a *soubrette.* Sort of a cutie-pie singer and dancer. Finally I became the star myself."

Wow, thought Sister. Who needs a brain

VAUDEVILLE?

surgeon or a marathon runner? *"You were on the stage?"* she said. "Did you sing and dance? Were you a...cutie pie?"

Gran chuckled. "I had my moments. At least, Roscoe the Red-Nosed Clown thought so. But no, not really—I didn't have that kind of talent. I was known as Wanda the One-Bear Band. 'Wanda' was a stage name, of course."

Questions tumbled into Sister's mind so fast that she couldn't seem to get them out of her mouth. Gran smiled. She understood why Sister was speechless. She went over to a dusty shelf and took down something wrapped in a plastic bag. Then she shook off the dust and unwrapped it. It was an old picture album. Gran brought the album over to Sister and opened it to a poster of herself as Wanda the One-Bear Band.

What a sight! There was Gran—much, much younger, of course. She was wearing tights and holding a saxophone. But that wasn't all. She had a harmonica in her mouth and a drum and cymbals strapped to her waist. A bicycle horn was attached to the drum. And she was on *roller skates!*

For a while, Sister just stared wide-eyed at the poster. Finally she asked, "Could you really play all those instruments?"

"Not well," said Gran, "but *loud*. It didn't really matter much, though. The roller skates made such a racket on the wooden stage that you could hardly hear the music, anyway. And I was a terrific skater."

Sister could believe it. She knew that Gran was an excellent ice skater. Gran had even been referee for one of Brother's ice hockey games last winter.

"That's fantastic, Gran!" said Sister. "Just fantastic!"

"Well, will I do?" asked Gran.

"Do what?"

"Will I do as the subject of your oral history project?"

"You'll be great!" cried Sister. "You'll be terrific! It'll be the best oral history in

the whole class! But Gran..."

"Yes?"

"Where's your stage stuff—your costume and all? And who was Roscoe the Red-Nosed Clown?"

"The costume's up here somewhere," said Gran. "As for Roscoe...we'll talk about him next time. You'd best be getting home for dinner, dear."

Chapter 5
A Small Mystery

As Sister walked home from Gran's, her mind was full of unusual words like "vaudeville," "headliner," and "soubrette." She kept thinking about Gran's amazing past. The most amazing thing of all was to imagine Gran as Wanda the One-Bear Band.

Until that afternoon, Sister had always thought of Gran as...well, just Gran. A wonderful Gran whom she loved, of course. A Gran who made delicious cookies and grew beautiful flowers, who was always there when you needed her. But now, after her visit to Gran's attic, Sister was sure that Gran was perfect for her oral history project.

Sister wanted to tell Mama about her visit with Gran as soon as she got home. But Mama was on the phone. So Sister plumped herself down on the sofa and waited for her to finish her call. She wondered if Mama knew about Gran's vaudeville days. It seemed kind of odd that neither Mama nor Papa had ever said anything about them.

Mama had a long list of calls to make. At one point she turned to Sister and asked her how she'd made out with Gran. Sister said, "Okay." But before she could say another word, Mama was back on the phone.

Sister couldn't help hearing Mama's end of the phone conversations. Mama was a member of the Bear Country Parent-

Teacher Association, and she had been put in charge of finding acts for the big talent show. This wasn't as easy as it sounded. Mama worked hard on the phone, like a real salesbear. She kept saying things like "the school really needs money," "*any* sort of talent," "it's all in fun," and "valuable prizes!"

After a while, it began to look as if Mama wasn't going to be done on the phone any-

time soon. So Sister went out to Papa's woodworking shop to tell him about Gran's amazing past.

But Papa was busy too. Squire Grizzly was there with his fancy carved walking stick and snazzy clothes. He wanted Papa to copy one of his most prized antique tables. Squire Grizzly was Papa's biggest customer, so Sister didn't interrupt. With Brother nowhere in sight, she realized that her story about Gran would have to wait.

Now, it's a funny thing about stories you're eager to tell. Often, if you don't get to tell them right away, they quickly begin to feel less urgent. That's exactly what happened to Sister's story about Gran. In fact, it wasn't until she and Brother were doing their homework that evening that she finally brought the subject up. Brother was very impressed with what she told him about Gran's past.

"You know, Sis," he said, taking his science book out of his backpack, "we cubs shouldn't think of older folks like Gran as boring or 'over the hill.' Come to think of it, being 'over the hill' shouldn't make folks boring anyway. To be 'over the hill,' you have to have *climbed* the hill."

Wow, Brother thought. Wanda the One-Bear Band. Fantastic! But why hadn't

Mama or Papa ever said anything about it?

Later, while the cubs were getting ready for bed, Brother had a great idea. He stopped right in the middle of brushing his teeth and called to Sister. She came to the bathroom in her pajamas.

"What's the matter?" she asked.

"Nothing," said Brother. Toothpaste was all over his lower lip. "I just had a great idea. Gran could enter the big PTA talent

I JUST HAD A GREAT IDEA.

show! She'd be a big hit with her one-bear-band act!"

Sister frowned. "I don't know about that," she said. "Gran's pretty old. She might not be able to do the act anymore."

"Of course she can do it," said Brother. "You saw her ref that hockey game, didn't you? She was the best skater on the ice."

"Hmm," said Sister. "Maybe you're right."

"You bet I'm right," said Brother. "Tomorrow morning I'll tell Mama to give Gran a call."

"No, wait," said Sister quickly. "Better not."

"Why not?"

"If you tell Mama about the idea, she'll tell Papa," said Sister. "Don't you think he might be embarrassed about his own mother appearing as Wanda the One-Bear Band?"

"You could be right," said Brother, nodding. "Guess it's safer not to mention it. But I still think Gran would be a hit in the talent show."

So do I, thought Sister as she climbed into bed and pulled the covers up to her chin. Would Gran really do it after all these years? Probably not. But it wouldn't hurt to ask...

Sister remembered that her next interview with Gran was tomorrow after school. As she drifted toward sleep, she decided to take the talent show notice with her to Gran's.

Chapter 6
Class Announcements

The next morning at breakfast, Mama told Papa and the cubs about the great acts she had signed up for the talent show. Brother and Sister were surprised to hear how talented the citizens of Bear Country were. They had never known that Teacher Bob

could juggle and do magic tricks. Or that Lizzy Bruin's dad could play country fiddle. It was also news to them that Police Chief Bruno and three of his officers could sing barbershop quartet. As surprised as they were by Mama's talent list, the cubs wanted to say out loud that Gran's talent was still the most unusual of all. But they kept it to themselves.

That day, after morning recess, Teacher Jane asked for the names of all the bears who would be interviewed for the oral history project. Several hands shot up right away.

I WANT A GIRL -- JUST LIKE THE GIRL -- WHO MARRIED DEAR OLD DAD!

Lizzy Bruin announced her choice of the uncle who was a brain surgeon. There were "oohs" from her classmates. Queenie McBear announced her choice—her marathon-winning aunt. There were "aahs." And when Tim Honeypot said he had chosen His Honor the Mayor, there was even applause.

One by one, the rest of the class announced their choices. Everyone seemed to have found someone who sounded interesting. At last Teacher Jane called on Sister Bear. "And whom have you chosen, Sister?" she asked.

Sister sat straight in her chair and in a loud, clear voice said, "My grandmother."

The class tittered. Some of the cubs made faces at each other.

"Your *grandmother?*" said Teacher Jane. She looked disappointed. "Grizzly Gran is a nice old bear, Sister. But is she really the best subject you can think of?"

"Yes, ma'am," said Sister.

There were more titters and a few groans.

But Sister only smiled. Boy, she thought, are *they* in for a surprise!

Chapter 7
A Major Disagreement

The door to Gran's house was unlocked when Sister got there. So she walked right in and called, "Anyone home?"

"In here, dear," called Gramps from his study.

Sister wondered what Gramps was working on today. He had lots of hobbies. He spent many hours dry-fly tying, carving monkeys from peach pits, and writing angry letters to the government.

But today Gramps was hard at work on his favorite hobby: building model ships in bottles. It was very delicate work that took lots of concentration. So at first Gramps didn't notice that Sister had come into the room.

Sister smiled as she watched Gramps work. Some folks said Gramps was a solid, steady sort of fellow. Others, including Gran, said he was something of a stick-in-the-mud who was too set in his ways.

But to Sister, Gramps was just a wonderful grandfather. Sure, sometimes he was grouchy and grumbly. But he was also very lovable. And he was always ready to spend time with Brother and Sister.

"Great-looking ship, Gramps," said Sister.

"Oh, hi, dear," said Gramps. "Thanks. First four-masted schooner I ever tried."

"Is Gran around?"

"Up in the attic doing goodness-knows-what," said Gramps. "She said to go on up."

Sister climbed the stairs to the attic. When she reached the door, she got something of a shock. She was used to seeing Gran in her usual plain housedress. But instead, there was Gran, dressed in the costume of Wanda the One-Bear Band. She wore a pink-spangled body suit and had all of the one-bear band rig—harmonica, saxophone, drum with cymbals, and bicycle

horn. She was even wearing roller skates.

"*Ta-da!*" said Gran. She also wore a proud grin.

"Wow!" cried Sister. "Positively humongous!"

"Is that good?" asked Gran.

"*Good?*" said Sister. "It's...humongous!" Sister went up to Gran and examined everything. "This is really awesome, Gran," she said. "And it still fits! You're exactly the size you were when you were younger. Oh, by the way, here's a notice I brought from school. There's going to be a big PTA talent show. Brother and I think you should enter. You'd be a real hit!"

THE WEEK FOR TWO AT GRIZZLYLAND SOUNDS GREAT.

Gran put on her glasses to read the notice. "Yes, I might be at that," she said. Then she shook her head. "But I really don't think..."

Suddenly Gran's eyes lit up. "Hey, look at this list of prizes. Dinner for two, a gift certificate, a case of honey....The week for two at Grizzlyland sounds great. It might loosen up old stick-in-the-mud Gramps a little. But no, I really don't think..."

"Aw, come on, Gran," said Sister. "It would sure show the cubs in my class. They...well, they giggled when I said I was interviewing you for my oral history."

Gran frowned. "Giggled, did they?"

"It would show everyone that older folks can *do* things," said Sister.

Gran thought for a moment. "Heck," she said, "I don't even know if I can still work this rig..."

Gran tested the harmonica. Then she blew a note on the sax. Both sounded fine. Pretty soon she was into her old Wanda act. She wailed a tune on the sax and harmonica, beat the drum, crashed the cymbals, honked the bicycle horn, and skated up a storm. The noise was tremendous!

"Go, Gran!" cried Sister. "Go! Go! Go!"

In an instant, Gramps was at the door, gasping for breath from his dash upstairs. He glared at Gran, who stopped playing and skating the moment she saw him.

"I don't believe it!" barked Gramps. "You scared me half to death with that racket! Sounded like the world was coming to an end! Shook the house like an earthquake!"

"I'm sorry, dear," said Gran. "It was thoughtless of me. I certainly didn't mean to frighten you."

"Frighten me?" said Gramps. "Ha! It'll take more than a giddy old grandma on roller skates who doesn't know how to act her age to frighten *me*..." Just then he saw the talent show notice lying on the card table. He picked it up. "What's this?"

Sister had never seen Gramps so angry with Gran. She hardly knew what to think or do. Quickly she said, "It's really my fault, Gramps. You see, we have this oral history assignment at school, and..."

But Gramps wasn't listening. He was reading the talent show notice. Then he looked up at Gran with an angry look in his eyes. "Don't tell me you're even *thinking* about entering this talent show," he said.

"Says here anyone over twenty-one can enter. You're over twenty-one, all right. *Way* over. Now listen to me, Mrs. Giddy Grandma. You can *forget* about entering this show, because..." Gramps stopped for a breath. He was so angry he could hardly speak.

"Because what?" said Gran. She glared right back.

"Because I absolutely, totally, and completely forbid it! Get that? Forbid it, forbid it, forbid it!"

With that, Gramps turned and stomped out of the attic. Gran and Sister could hear his heavy footsteps going down the stairs.

Sister was very worried. She was beginning to wish she had never shown Gran the notice. "Gran," she said, "I don't think..."

But Gran was still glaring at the attic doorway. "Now, *I like that!*" she said. "Forbid it, does he? Well, I'll show that stick-in-the-mud old fogey. Sister, how do you get into this talent show?"

"Just call Mama," said Sister. "She's in charge. But, Gran, don't you think...?"

"Help me out of this rig!" ordered Gran. "I've got a telephone call to make."

Chapter 8
A Secret from the Past?

When Sister got home from Gran's, Mama was waiting for her in the living room with a worried look on her face.

"What in the world is going on over at Gran's?" Mama asked Sister.

"Did she call you?" asked Sister.

"Yes," said Mama. "She signed up for the talent show. How can she be serious? Even *thinking* about bringing back the old Wanda act..."

Sister told Mama what had happened at Gran's. Mama shook her head sadly and sighed. "Oh, dear!" she said. "That's awful!"

Papa looked up from his newspaper. "What's so awful about it?" he said. "So Gran wants to have a little fun. Why should Gramps have a problem with that?"

"Are you forgetting why the Wanda act makes Gramps so upset?" asked Mama. Suddenly she remembered that Brother and Sister were listening. "Little pitchers have big ears," she told Papa. She motioned for him to follow her to the kitchen.

"Little pitchers—that's us," said Brother when he and Sister were alone in the living room. They tried as hard as they could to hear the lowered voices coming from the kitchen. But it was no use.

"How do you like that?" said Sister. "Papa wasn't angry at all about Gran's act. But Gramps sure was."

"Something really bad must have happened way back then," said Brother. "Some deep, dark secret…Hey, Sis?"

"What?"

"How was Wanda the One-Bear Band?"

Sister's face broke into a broad grin. "You should have seen her," she said. "She was *sen-SA-tional!*"

Chapter 9
The Secret Revealed

The next afternoon, when Sister arrived at Gran's for another interview, she found a note in the front hall telling her to come up to the attic. She was glad to see it. All day she had been worrying about running into Gramps downstairs.

I sure hope Gramps doesn't blame me for all of this, Sister thought as she tiptoed upstairs. She loved Gramps very much and didn't want to be the cause of something so upsetting to him.

Gran had some things to show Sister in the attic. She placed a couple of chairs side by side and opened a big album of photos and clippings while Sister turned on her tape recorder.

"How did you meet Gramps?" asked Sister, sitting down beside Gran. "Was he in vaudeville too?"

"Heavens, no," said Gran. "He was a 'stage-door Johnny.' That's what we called fellows who waited at the stage door to see the performers."

"Did he see you on stage and fall in love with you?" asked Sister.

"I guess you might say so," said Gran.

She pointed to a picture in the album. "Here we are on our first date at Fun Park."

"Hey, Gramps was pretty cute," said Sister.

"Still is," said Gran. "Grumpy, but cute."

Sister stared for a while at the photo. It

HERE WE ARE ON OUR FIRST DATE AT FUN PARK.

was strange thinking about Gramps and Gran as a romantic young couple. But the photo showed that they surely had been. Then Sister noticed a photo of Gran with another good-looking fellow. "Who's that?" she asked.

"That's Roscoe the Red-Nosed Clown," said Gran. "Out of costume, of course."

"He's pretty cute too."

"Roscoe was our closing act," said Gran. "Now here he is in his clown getup, riding a unicycle."

"Were Gramps and Roscoe rivals?" asked Sister.

Gran smiled. "Were they ever! I just about had to beat them off with a stick..." Her smile vanished. "That's what all this

fuss is about. Can you believe it? Gramps is downstairs sulking about something that happened more than forty years ago."

"So, what happened?" asked Sister. She began looking through the album.

"Well, I guess it was partly my fault," said Gran. "I was sort of dating both of them. It happened at a Saturday night dance at the town hall. Everyone was there—that's what

made it so awful. I was there with Roscoe.
And Gramps was there by himself. When
Gramps saw me dancing with Roscoe, he
tried to cut in. He must have tapped
Roscoe a little too hard on the shoulder.
Roscoe shoved him, and Gramps took a fall.

"Well, the floor had been waxed that day,
and the fall Gramps took was a big arm-
waving, slip-sliding one—WHAMMO!—

right smack onto the floor. The band stopped playing, and everybody stopped dancing to see what would happen. We all knew that Gramps wasn't a guy to fool with."

Sister closed the album and looked wide-eyed up at Gran. "Did they fight?" she asked.

"Worse," said Gran. "*Much* worse. Gramps picked himself up off the floor and went up to Roscoe. Then he slapped Roscoe in the face and challenged him to a duel."

"A *duel?*"

"I know it sounds crazy," said Gran. "But you have to remember—this was a long time ago. Duels were illegal back then, just as they are now, but they still happened from time to time."

Sister was on the edge of her seat. "And what happened?" she asked.

"Well, the rule of the duel is that the one who is challenged gets to choose the weapons."

"What did Roscoe choose?" asked Sister. "Swords? Guns?"

"Neither," said Gran. "Roscoe chose *pies*. Cream-filled pies at three paces. And wouldn't you know it, some smarty went across the street to Grizzburger's Bakery and brought back two cream pies."

"And did they duel?" asked Sister.

"Right then and there. Now, since Roscoe

was a clown, he was an expert pie thrower. Before Gramps could even take aim, Roscoe let loose and whammed him right in the face with one. Gramps was all covered with goo. Some of it got on the floor, and Gramps slipped in it and took an even worse fall than before. Of course, every-body thought it was hilarious. You've never heard such laughter, including mine. But even as Gramps slunk off the dance floor, covered with pie, I knew he was the one I loved.

"He wouldn't speak to me for weeks. We finally did get together, though, and ended up getting married. But I guess he never really got over that whole business with Roscoe. That's why he's all in an uproar about me being in the talent show."

Gran stood up, walked to the window, and looked off into the distance.

"Maybe you shouldn't be in the talent show," said Sister.

Gran shook her head. "That's not the answer, dear. He's got to get off his high horse and get over this foolishness. There's such a thing as letting bygones be bygones, you know. And there's also such a thing as being a good sport. Nope. I'm doing Wanda in the talent show come heck or high water."

Just then something in the front yard caught Gran's eye. "Uh-oh!" she said.

Sister hurried to the window and looked down. Gramps was leaving the house. And he was carrying a pair of suitcases.

"Oh, no!" cried Sister. "Gramps is moving out!"

Gran held her breath as Gramps trudged across the yard. But when he passed his pickup truck in the driveway, she let out a sigh of relief. Gramps was moving out, all right. But he was moving only as far as the garden shed.

Sister broke off her interview with Gran and hurried home. It was clear to her now why Mama and Papa had been so worried when Gran had signed up for the talent show. As soon as she got home, Sister told Mama and Papa what Gramps had done.

"Moved out?" gasped Mama. "Oh, dear! Oh, dear!"

"Just into the garden shed," said Sister.

Mama sighed. "Thank goodness for that," she said. "But I'm still very worried."

Papa stroked his chin as he thought. "Maybe we can change Gramps's mind about Gran and the talent show," he said.

"I don't think so," said Sister. "According to Gran, he's still every bit as angry now about Roscoe as he was forty years ago."

"She told you about that, did she?" said Papa.

"It's all right here," said Sister, patting her tape recorder. "I don't know what's going to happen between Gramps and Gran. But I do know I'm going to have the greatest oral history in the history of oral history."

Chapter 10
Rarin' to Go

As the day of the big talent show approached, there was no change in the standoff between Gramps and Gran. Mama begged Gran to forget about the talent show. And Papa tried to convince Gramps

to forget about his long-ago problems with Roscoe the Red-Nosed Clown. But none of Mama's begging or Papa's convincing seemed to do any good.

"Age is a matter of mind over matter," Gran told Mama. "And it's mind that matters. As you get older, you've got to get out and *do* things. Otherwise you can get stuck deeper and deeper in the mud. That's the problem with Gramps: his get-up-and-go got up and went!"

Meanwhile, Gramps told Papa, "Gran's got to act her age and not go out of her way to make a fool of herself!"

And Gramps kept right on living out in the garden shed, while Gran kept right on practicing her Wanda act up in the attic.

At last the big day came. Mama arrived at the school auditorium early to get things ready backstage. Brother and Sister came along to help. Later, Papa picked up Gran and drove her to school.

Already music filled the auditorium as everyone warmed up their instruments and singing voices. Lizzy Bruin's dad scraped away on his fiddle. Chief Bruno and the rest of his barbershop quartet worked on their harmonies. Someone's saxophone whined. A snare drum rattled.

Teacher Jane's shoes clacked on the wooden floor as she practiced her tap-dance routine. About the only one who wasn't making a racket was Teacher Bob, who was juggling four red balls.

Mama noticed Gran and Papa and hurried over to greet them. "I was worried you'd be late, Gran," she said. "You're the last to arrive."

"I wanted to get in some last-minute practice all by myself up in the attic," said Gran. "No need to worry. I'm rarin' to go!"

"What about Gramps?" asked Mama, lowering her voice. "Any change?"

"Still in the doghouse," said Gran with a frown. "Or the garden shed, to be exact. He's a stubborn old mule, that one." Then she smiled and looked from Mama to Papa to Sister. "At least the rest of my family is here to see me win the big talent show."

Papa looked around and said, "Except for Brother. Where is he?"

Puzzled, Mama looked around too. "He was here a few minutes ago...," she said.

"Where did he go?" asked Sister.

"Don't worry," said Gran. "I'm sure he'll turn up."

Chapter 11
One Last Chance

Brother Bear was on his way to Gramps and Gran's. He wanted one last chance to talk Gramps into swallowing his pride and forgetting about his run-in with Roscoe the Red-Nosed Clown.

At least Gramps could be a good sport and come to the show, thought Brother as he walked along. After all, *he* was the one who got Gran, not Roscoe.

When Brother reached Gramps and Gran's, he went straight to the garden shed. He knocked on the door and waited. But no one came to the door.

"Gramps!" he called. "It's me, Brother!"

Still no one answered.

Brother tried the doorknob. It turned, and the door swung open. Inside were rakes and hoes and shovels standing in corners. Other gardening tools hung on a pegboard along one wall. There was a workbench, with an old-fashioned lawnmower leaning against it.

But Gramps wasn't there. And none of his belongings were there, either. Brother looked back at the driveway. The pickup truck was gone! Oh, no, thought Brother. He's really left this time.

Brother walked slowly to the front porch and sat down on the steps. He put his head in his hands and stared at the ground. It just didn't seem possible. After forty years of marriage, Gramps and Gran were breaking up.

Brother thought about what must be going on at school right at that moment. When he had left, the excitement was building. A large group had just arrived by bus from the Golden Age Home to see Gran's act. By now the show was probably on. The auditorium was probably packed, with standing room only. And Gran, the last to perform, must be eagerly waiting for her turn. Brother wondered if she knew that Gramps had moved out of the garden shed.

Brother was about to head back to school with the bad news about Gramps when he heard something coming down the road. He jumped up for a better look and saw Gramps in his pickup truck.

Good! thought Brother. Gramps must have forgotten something and come back to get it!

WELL, WELL, IF IT ISN'T—

Brother ran to meet the truck as it pulled into the driveway. He would get his chance to speak to Gramps, after all. He knew he had to talk Gramps into staying!

"Well, well, if it isn't—" Gramps said as he climbed down from the truck.

But Brother cut him off. "Now don't say a word, Gramps—just listen to me. What you're doing to Gran isn't fair."

"But—" said Gramps.

"No 'buts'! That business with Roscoe happened more than forty years ago. It's time you forgot all about it."

"But—" said Gramps.

"And even if it happened last week," said Brother, "that's no reason to keep Gran from doing her Wanda act. You may have lost the duel, but you won Gran over. Gran loves *you*, Gramps, not Roscoe!"

"Now hold on!" cried Gramps, waving his

arms in the air. "I'm not gonna argue with you."

"You're not?" said Brother.

"Nope," said Gramps. "I agree with you. That's what I've been trying to tell you. But you wouldn't let me get a word in edgewise. I know I've been an awful fool. But I'm gonna make up for it. Look here—" He pointed to a unicycle and an outfit in the back of the truck. "I just rented them over in Big Bear City. That's a red-nosed clown suit you're looking at."

"Clown suit?" said Brother. "What're you going to do, Gramps?"

"I'm going to the show," said Gramps. "And I'm going to help your Gran out."

"Great!" cried Brother. "Gran's act is the last one. If we hurry, we can still catch it."

Gramps climbed back into the truck. "Let's go," he said. "But first we've got to

stop by Grizzburger's Bakery and pick up a couple of props."

"Props?" said Brother.

"Things to use in the show," said Gramps. "And you and Sister are going to be in charge of them."

"What do we have to do?" asked Brother.

Gramps opened the door for Brother. "Hop in," he said. "I'll tell you on the way."

Chapter 12
Band Meets Clown

Gran was just beginning her act when Gramps and Brother arrived. They hurried backstage.

All the acts were good, but many in the audience had come just to see Wanda the One-Bear Band. There were cheers and

whistles as Gran skated in a graceful figure eight, beating the drum and crashing the cymbals. Soon she added the saxophone, harmonica, and bicycle horn. Then, still doing a figure eight, she turned on her skates and began skating backward.

The audience loved the act. They went wild. Some began applauding when it was only half over. And when Gran went into her final spin, the entire audience rose for a standing ovation. Gran spun to a stop in the center of the stage and spread her arms to receive the applause.

But, to everyone's surprise, the act wasn't over! Out of the wings came another performer—a red-nosed clown riding a unicycle.

When Gran saw the clown, her mouth fell open in surprise. It looked just like Roscoe the Red-Nosed Clown! But no, it couldn't be!

Gran skated to the side of the stage to give the clown room to perform. She stood staring at him. It took her only a moment to figure out who it was. It was Gramps! Her own Gramps was all dressed up like Roscoe!

A big smile spread across Gran's face as she watched Gramps cycle in a circle. She knew this was his way of telling her that he had finally gotten over his duel with Roscoe. And she knew that he was just as much in love with her now as he had been when he first saw Wanda the One-Bear

Band more than forty years ago.

Suddenly Gramps stopped circling and looked over at someone in the wings. Brother Bear ran out and handed something to Gramps.

Gasps and shrieks rose from the audience. What is it? thought Gran. Good grief! It was a pie—a great big cream-filled pie— and Gramps was coming right at her with it!

SPLOOSH!

"Gran!" called a high voice from the wings on her side of the stage. "Take this!"

Sister Bear darted out with a second cream pie, and handed it to Gran.

As the shrieks from the audience grew louder, Gran skated to meet Gramps at center stage. They faced each other and began circling...they raised their pies...then... SPLOOSH! Both pies hit their marks at the same instant.

SPLOOSH!

The audience screamed with laughter. Gramps and Gran, faces covered with cream, slipped and slid in the goo that had fallen to the stage. Finally they fell to the floor in a pie-smeared bear hug and kiss. The audience went wild.

Off in the wings, Sister Bear beamed. Gramps and Gran had gotten back together! And Sister knew that she was sure to get an A-plus for the best oral history in the history of oral history.

Gran won first prize for her one-bear-band act, of course. And can you guess which prize she chose from the list?

Stan and Jan Berenstain began writing and illustrating books for children in the early 1960s, when their two young sons were beginning to read. That marked the start of the best-selling Berenstain Bears series. Now, with more than one hundred books in print, videos, television shows, and even Berenstain Bears attractions at major amusement parks, it's hard to tell where the Bears end and the Berenstains begin!

Stan and Jan make their home in Bucks County, Pennsylvania, near their sons—Leo, a writer, and Michael, an illustrator—who are helping them with Big Chapter Books stories and pictures. They plan on writing and illustrating many more books for children, especially for their four grand-children, who keep them well in touch with the kids of today.